Will you count the stars without me?

Will you count the stars without me?

STORY AND WATERCOLORS BY
Jane Breskin Zalben

Farrar · Straus · Giroux · New York

Copyright © 1979 Jane Breskin Zalben
All rights reserved
Published simultaneously in Canada by McGraw-Hill Ryerson Ltd., Toronto
The text is set in Weiss Roman from the Royal Composing Room
Printed in the United States of America by A. Hoen
Color separations by Offset Separations Corp.
Bound by A. Horowitz and Son
Designed by Jane Breskin Zalben
First edition, 1979
Library of Congress Cataloging in Publication Data
Zalben, Jane Breskin.   Will you count the stars without me?
[1. Animals—Fiction.   2. Islands—Fiction]   I. Title.
PZ7.Z254Wi   [E]   78-16069   isbn 0-374-38433-9

To Celia Mitchell,
who grows flowers in the winter,
and knows how to be a happy, whole,
independent human being

Saba and Shana live on an island.
They sleep in a palm tree
close to the stars.
Sometimes they try to count them,
whispering until dawn.
They have everything
they could want or need.
A little stream of fresh water,
banana, date, and fig trees,
the sun, the moon, the stars,
their friends in the jungle,
and, of course, each other.

One year there was too much rain.
The bananas, the dates, and the figs
didn't grow. There was little to eat.
Everyone gathered together.
Shana said bravely, "I'll search for food."

Saba lowered his eyes. "Don't go,"
he thought, but instead he said,
"We've never been apart. I'll miss you."
"I'll miss you, too," said Shana.
But she left that morning before sunrise.

Saba watched the boat sail away.
A tear slipped down his cheek.
He took a deep breath and sighed.

He sat on a rock and stared at the ocean.
Saba was sure he wouldn't have
a good time until Shana came home.

He didn't even look up when his friends
Otto and Lilly came by and sat on the rock
next to him. "Come on," they said.
"Help us build our new wallow."

"I don't feel like it," said Saba.

So Otto and Lilly went off by themselves.

Saba could hear them giggling and digging.

He had never felt so lonely.

All day he paced back and forth
across the island.

He wondered if she'd find the last coconut
he hid between her pajama top and bottom.

And that night he lay awake thinking,
"Will you count the stars without me?"
He stared at the empty spot beside him.
Finally he fell asleep.

The morning breeze brought
the smell of the sea and
Otto's and Lilly's voices.
Their laughter became louder and louder.

When he couldn't stand it any longer,
he stumped down the path. "Stop giggling!"
"What's the matter, Saba?"
"Shana went away. She went away without me."

Saba glumly watched Otto and Lilly dig.
After a while he said, "I don't think you're digging
deep enough." He jumped down and showed them.
He spent the whole afternoon digging.

Then Cecil came along and asked Saba
to carve a weathervane out of an old
coconut shell into the shape of a banana.

As the stars came out,
he curled up and thought,
"I had a nice day."

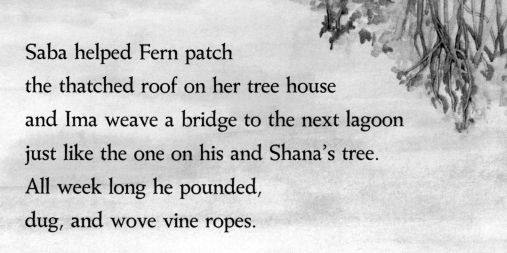

Saba helped Fern patch
the thatched roof on her tree house
and Ima weave a bridge to the next lagoon
just like the one on his and Shana's tree.
All week long he pounded,
dug, and wove vine ropes.

At the end of the week,
the animals rested on
the sand in the hot sun.

The waves cooled their toes.
It was getting dark when
Shana's boat drifted onto shore.

"Saba!" yelled Shana.

"Shana!" yelled Saba.

All the animals cheered, "Yea for Shana!"

Saba and Shana hugged each other tightly.

"How are you?" he asked.

"Very happy," said Shana.

"I'm glad I could help my friends.
What have you been doing?"
"Come on, I'll show you," Saba said.
He took her by the hand and smiled.
Shana could take care of herself.
And so could he.

And they stayed up the whole night
counting the stars and eating coconuts.